THE
CAT SITTER MYSTERY

THE
CAT SITTER
MYSTERY

CAROL ADORJAN

AN AVON CAMELOT BOOK

AVON BOOKS
A division of
The Hearst Corporation
105 Madison Avenue
New York, New York 10016

Library of Congress Cataloging in Publication Data

Adorjan, Carol Madden.
  The cat sitter mystery.

  Summary: Is the old lady next door a witch? This
and other problems keep Beth busy the rest of the
summer in her new home.
  [1. Mystery and detective stories] I. Title.
Pz7.A2618Cat   1986   [Fic]   85-15819

First Camelot Printing, January 1986

For
Beth, who's been there,
and Elisa and Marjorie,
who helped me find the way.

Chapter One

Beth Carew followed the black cat through a tunnel of branches and came out next door. Immediately, she felt uneasy—as if someone were watching her. She thought she saw a flash of movement. She looked up at the old house. The long narrow windows looked back, blank and unseeing.

The cat wove between her ankles, purring insistently. Beth stooped to stroke it, never taking her eyes from the tall, narrow house. Set far back on the lot, surrounded by bushes, it was much larger than she had thought. And scary. With the clouds moving behind it, it seemed to be falling toward her. It did lean forward, bent with age and decay, its gray paint faded and wrinkled. A fitting house for a black cat, she thought.

A shadow fell across her, and a voice said, "I see you've found O.C."

Startled, Beth glanced up. A tall, thin woman towered above her. Her sun-darkened skin was lined like old leather, and her electric hair was bright red except at the roots where it was dull green. She and the house were obviously related.

"Name's Sibyl Goodall," the woman said. "You're?"

"Beth Carew." Beth gathered the cat to her and stood. Under her long hair, her skin prickled. Even with her

1

back to the house, she knew someone was watching them. She wondered if she should mention it, but instead, she said, "We just moved in—"

"Next door. Yes. I saw the moving van. We're happy to have you, aren't we, O.C.?"

"O.C.?"

"It's short for Other Cat."

"Other Cat? Do you have more than one?"

"Indeed yes! There's Cat, who came first. Just wandered in and never left. He must have sent word out somehow and the others descended." She laughed a curious, tinkling laugh as pleasant as wind chimes. "For a while I thought it was raining cats. O.C. was next. Sometime later I found F.C. in a box outside the back door shivering with fright."

"F.C.," Beth repeated. "Fraidy Cat?"

"Yes. Still is a timid little thing. There's C.C., of course. A neighbor brought her in wrapped in newspapers. I call her Copy Cat." Mrs. Goodall chuckled. "Funny, I never liked cats. Too independent for my taste. I never could tell what they were thinking. And there I was with a good start on an alphabet full of them."

O.C. squirmed. Beth squatted and the cat poured out of her arms onto the grass.

"Never liked them and there I was with five."

"Five?"

"L.C. Last Cat."

Mrs. Goodall emphasized *last* in such a hopeful, almost pleading way that Beth began to laugh.

"You're sure about that?" she asked.

"Never sure about anything." The woman studied Beth

as if she were seeing her for the first time. "You like cats," she said.

"Oh, yes! Better than anything except horses, but I can't have a cat because my father's allergic."

Mrs. Goodall shook her head sympathetically, but her eyes had glazed over, and Beth was certain she hadn't heard her. "You wouldn't be afraid, would you?" she asked.

Beth shifted uneasily. "Afraid?" She hoped Mrs. Goodall didn't hear the quaver in her voice. "What's there to be afraid of?"

"Nothing really. It's a lovely old house. I grew up in it, you know. But sometimes . . ." Her voice trailed off.

"My mother and father say old houses have more personality than newer ones," Beth put in.

Mrs. Goodall laughed. "This one certainly has a mind of its own—like a member of the family—and it can be very perverse." She clapped her hands and O.C. leaped into her arms. "Perhaps you and I could be useful to one another, my dear." She carried the cat toward the house, muttering, "Yes. That might be a good idea. A very good idea indeed."

Watching Mrs. Goodall approach the open front porch, Beth wondered if she would be afraid alone in that strange, silent house, and why the woman had asked.

Suddenly, in a third floor dormer window, something moved. A cat. Beth smiled. So that's what had been watching them: the eyes of a cat. Then a hand reached out and grasped the cat. The animal's mouth opened in a silent cry. Above it, an enormous masklike face appeared.

3

Beth gasped. She urged herself to run, but she was rooted to the spot.

Across the hedge, a truck whirred, a door slammed. Beth's twin brother and sister giggled. Her mother called, "Beth!"

Still, she couldn't move.

Then, as suddenly as they had appeared, cat and face dropped from sight.

The spell broken, Beth scrambled under the bushes. In her own garden, the twins Katie and John toddled after a bluejay. Overhead a black squirrel chattered.

"There you are, Babe!" Mrs. Carew said. "Exploring?"

Too upset to speak, Beth nodded.

"Don't look now," her mother said, "but I think you've been followed."

Beth turned. O.C. lurked under the bushes, peering at her.

"Better take the cat back where it came from," her mother said. "Then I could do with your help. The movers just left, and there's a lot to do."

Beth crawled in after O.C. "I thought Mrs. Goodall took you in."

The minute she was on the other side of the hedge, her heart pounded and her palms went wet and sticky. It's like entering another world, she thought.

With her head down to avoid looking at the house, she ran to the porch, holding the cat tight against her like a football. She dropped O.C. on the steps. "Now stay there," she called as she sprinted back across the lawn.

At the hedge, she glanced back expecting to see that ghostly face. The long narrow windows peered down at her, blinking only tree shadows and sunlight.

Chapter Two

Beth had little time the next few days to think about the house on the corner. Her own was mysterious enough.

"It's so big," Mr. Carew joked, "someone besides us could live in it, and we'd never know it!"

Beth wasn't so sure it was a joke. There were nine rooms, two baths, an attic, and all kinds of cupboards and cubbyholes—all of it laid out so that a person could easily come and go without anyone knowing. The kitchen alone had five doors and a staircase!

"It'd made a great movie set," Beth said. "Can't you just see people going in and out of doors, with everybody just missing everybody else?"

"Until they got to this one." Mrs. Carew tugged at the door to the basement. "The way it sticks, they'd all pile up behind it or pull the whole set down!"

Mr. Carew added Fix Basement Door to his long list of things that needed doing.

During the first week, the dishwasher leaked into the basement, the shower leaked into the pantry, and carpenter ants invaded the screen porch.

"Maybe the place is haunted by someone who doesn't want us to live here," Beth suggested.

"This place is haunted all right," Mr. Carew answered. "But it's not ghosts; it's neglect."

Neglect might explain some of it, but not the things that creaked in the night or the eerie animal sounds that seemed to come from inside the walls. During the day Beth tapped these walls in search of secret passages.

The only truly unexpected find was in the attic: a birds' nest three feet high!

"It must have belonged to an eagle!" Mr. Carew said when they discovered it.

"Really?" Beth scanned the attic for a large opening.

Her father smiled. "No. Not really. Probably wrens or sparrows. This isn't one nest. It's an accumulation of nests."

Mrs. Carew, whose head and shoulders were in the attic (the rest of her was on the ladder in a second floor cupboard), heard that remark. "Speaking of accumulation, Beth," she said lightly, "what about your room?"

Her room. Beth had found all kinds of excuses not to do anything about it. Getting settled seemed too big a job. It was a stranger's room, and she was a stranger in it. Besides, every time she went into it, she was drawn to the windows where she could look into Mrs. Goodall's garden. A tree blocked her view of the house, hiding the windows except for an occasional flash of reflected sun. She didn't know what she expected to see there, but each time, she had the feeling that something was about to happen. At night, after she'd turned off the light, she took one last look next door. Then she got into bed and turned her back on the unpacked boxes.

But if she didn't unpack them soon, her mother would, and the room would be all neat and orderly—not the way she liked it at all.

"No matter what I do to it, it'll never be like my other room," she told her mother.

"It is small," her mother said, completely missing the point. "But it's only temporary. When we begin decorating, you can have your choice of bedrooms."

"When will that be?" Beth asked.

"Don't hold your breath," her father answered, consulting his list. Decorating was at the bottom.

There was one consolation: she could do as she pleased with the room—even write on the brick-patterned wallpaper. Once she had unpacked her horse collection and stabled it on three long shelves, Beth felt a little more at home. She combined her newts—Fig, Newton, and Natasha—with the fish in the aquarium. Cheepy's cylindrical birdcage filled in a corner nicely, and most of her books fitted into an old bookcase she found in the basement. Her blue and green rug with the two lions on it looked much better here than in her other room, where it had been too small. Finally, Beth tacked some wild animal pictures over her bed and hung one mobile of eyes and one of feet from the ceiling.

By the time she was settled, Katie and John had learned to climb the stairs. They came into her room all wide eyes and grasping hands.

There wasn't a key, but her father installed a hook and eye high out of the babies' reach so that Beth's things would be safe from invasion.

Now it was bright and unusual and private. Wondering how it would look to someone coming into it for the first time, Beth closed her eyes. Then she opened them suddenly, hoping to catch the room and herself by surprise. But it didn't work.

7

Her mother came up to look. "It's very imaginative," she said, appraising the room.

Beth wasn't totally convinced. No matter what you do to it, she thought, a room is just a room until you can bring someone you like into it and say, "This is my room."

Chapter Three

"Mrs. Goodall's a witch," Tiffany Tanner said. Tiffany was six, and she lived across the street.

Beth scooped up five jacks and caught the red ball on the first bounce. "What makes you think she's a witch?"

"She has a black cat, doesn't she?"

"Lots of people have black cats, Tiffany."

"Maybe they're all witches," Tiffany said. "Besides, my mother says it's strange having all those cats. She must have hundreds."

"Five." Beth was so annoyed she hit a jack with the side of her hand.

"You moved one!" Tiffany smiled her wide, toothless smile. "My turn."

Beth dropped the ball and jacks into the little girl's cupped hand. It was going to be a long summer with no one but Tiffany around.

A power mower started up across the hedge.

"I'll bet that's Paul Kallin," Tiffany said. "He used to cut our grass too, until he told me to get lost one day." She ran over to the bushes and peered through. "That's who it is all right. That awful Paul Kallin." She tossed her head indignantly, but her sausage curls barely bounced.

Beth smiled. If she thought she could do it, she would have leaped the hedge that minute. Anyone who had the nerve to tell Tiffany Tanner to get lost deserved a handshake.

O.C. appeared and pounced toward the girls.

Tiffany jumped up. "I think my mother's calling me," she said as she raced out of the garden.

Beth scratched the cat behind the ears. O.C. closed his eyes and rolled his head from side to side under her hand. She couldn't understand how anybody could dislike cats or be afraid of them. Cats were beautiful creatures. Independent, as Mrs. Goodall had said, and wonderfully strange. They weren't solid like other animals. They seemed to go from one state to another—wafting along, barely touching firm ground one minute, and then going limp and boneless, pouring themselves into little puddles of fluff. If she could be any animal in the world, Beth would be a cat.

At the back door, Mrs. Carew asked, "How would you like to take the babies for a walk while I make dinner?"

"Sure," Beth answered. Pushing the stroller was not her favorite activity, but there was nothing better to do.

"Up that way a block or so, there's a girl about your age. I saw her yesterday on the way home from shopping."

Beth nodded and wheeled the stroller out of the drive.

"It's a yellow house with black shutters," her mother called.

Her mother was always after her to make new friends. As if it were all that easy. She didn't seem to realize you just couldn't go up to someone and say, "Hi, I'm Beth Carew." They might say, "So what?" or worse, they might say nothing at all.

Still, Beth turned north as her mother had directed.

10

She hoped Paul Kallin would see her and say "hi." Then she could ask him about the face she had seen in the window. But all Beth saw was a splotch of red moving steadily behind Mrs. Goodall's bushes.

By the time Beth turned toward home, the sun was as fuzzy as a ball of angora yarn. The air was heavy and still. Birds squawked overhead and squirrels chattered.

"It's going to rain," Beth said.

The babies looked skyward. "Wain, Wain, go 'way," they chanted.

As Beth pushed the buggy into the street, a bike sped around the corner. She yanked the twins back just in time.

"Hey! Watch where you're going!" Beth called after him. He flashed out of sight before Beth realized it was Paul Kallin.

It didn't rain all evening. For a while it looked as if it wouldn't rain at all. As she was getting ready for bed, Beth noticed how still and silent everything seemed—as though the world were holding its breath.

It wasn't until the Carews were all in bed that the wind began to whip the trees. Lightning flashed on and off as if someone were playing with a distant light switch. Thunder rumbled closer and closer like the footsteps of a giant. When the rain finally came, it fell straight and hard. It ran off the roof in sheets and spilled over the sides of the gutters.

Beth lay still watching the shadows shift and change. In the corner, Cheepy fell off his perch and landed on the bottom of the cage with a thud. Beth slipped out of bed, uncovered the cage, and lifted the door. She reached in and cupped the bird. His heart beat against her hand.

11

"Don't be afraid, little bird," she said softly, holding him against her cheek.

"Isn't this a storm?" Her mother stood at the bedroom door tying her robe. "I can't remember when there's been one like it."

Mr. Carew came up behind her. "It only seems worse because of all the trees." He was fiddling with a flashlight. "I'm going on down," he said, directing the beam toward the stairs.

"Are the lights out?" Beth asked.

"Yes," her mother answered. "And your father thinks the basement might be flooded. I'm going down to see if I can help. Would you like to come?"

"I don't think so." Beth set Cheepy on his perch. "I'll listen for the babies."

"I just checked them. They're sleeping like . . . babies. They'll probably sleep right through it." Thunder crashed. "You're sure you don't want to come down?"

"Thanks, but I'd rather stay here."

Her mother started down. "If you change your mind, we'll be in the basement."

Although she couldn't explain why, Beth was sure she wouldn't change her mind. Company would be comforting, but so was being alone in her own room, warm and cosy.

Suddenly, everything was light and sound. The house seemed to shake, and across the landing, Katie screamed.

Beth rushed to quieten her. Katie stood in her crib, rocking from one foot to the other. "Thun'er popped," she sobbed, clinging to her sister.

As Beth rubbed her small back, she felt Katie's heart beating as rapidly as her own.

John peeped through the slats of his crib. "Thun'er go 'way," he said, and then his eyes closed and he fell back to sleep.

Lightning flickered. Beth held her breath, waiting for the thunder. It sounded weakly, a distant rumble. The worst of the storm had passed. Katie settled on her stomach, sobbing softly.

In her own room, Beth opened a window wide. Her curtains fluttered. The mobiles spun dizzily. Outside, rain plunged through the drainpipes. The cool, fresh breeze sweetened the room with the heavy fragrance of flowers.

The best time in the world is after a storm, Beth thought.

Just then, lightning flashed. Leaves and grass glistened green in the white glare. Suddenly, a figure bolted across Mrs. Goodall's lawn. Something long and white flapped out behind it like giant wings.

Beth remembered Tiffany's voice saying, "Mrs. Goodall's a witch."

Her heart pounding in her ears, Beth dived into bed and pulled the covers over her head.

Chapter Four

"What would you do if something strange was going on somewhere?" Beth asked at breakfast. "Like next door for instance."

"Strange?" her mother said.

"You know: unexplainable."

Mr. Carew pushed back his chair. "Just because you don't know the explanation, doesn't mean there isn't one. Usually a—"

"Very simple one, right under a person's nose." Beth had heard that so many times she knew it by heart. "I know. But if you saw a face or something in a window. A large face I mean. Not an ordinary one. And then another time, you saw something all in white like a ghost. What would you do?"

"Have my eyes examined," Mr. Carew said. He circled the table, kissing each of them goodbye.

Beth sighed. It was difficult sometimes to have a father who made either a lecture or a joke out of everything. No one took her seriously. She knew they were busy with the babies and the house, but it was exasperating all the same.

The house on the corner was easily twice as big as her own. Maybe someone was living there unknown to Mrs. Goodall. If that were so, shouldn't she tell Mrs. Goodall?

14

But what if the woman already knew? What if whoever it was was a prisoner in the attic? Beth shuddered thinking what would happen then.

Later, as she coaxed the black squirrel out of his tree, she decided the whole thing was ridiculous. Anyone who would take in five homeless cats would not shut people in an attic. The only thing to do was go next door and tell Mrs. Goodall what she had seen. If the woman didn't know what was going on in her own house, she should be told. If she did know, there was probably a very simple explanation.

"Squirrels bite," Tiffany said, coming into the garden. "And sometimes they're rapid."

"Rapid?"

"You know. Diseased!"

"You mean *rabid*, Tiffany."

Tiffany shrugged. "Well, anyway, you could die."

The squirrel disappeared up the tree so Beth ate the nut she had been holding out to him.

Mrs. Carew came out with Katie and John. "Babe, Mrs. Goodall phoned. She'd like to see you."

Something dropped inside Beth like a flag of warning. It was one thing to say she was going to Mrs. Goodall's; it was another thing to go. "Did she say what she wanted?"

"No. Only that she wanted to talk to you."

Tiffany's brown eyes widened. "You're not going, are you?"

It was the same question Beth was asking herself. She said, "Of course I'm going. Why shouldn't I go?" The impatience in her voice was meant more for herself than for Tiffany.

"You wouldn't get me inside that house," Tiffany called

as Beth ducked through the hedge. "Not for a million trillion dollars."

No one answered the doorbell. Beth waited in the dark, clammy cool of Mrs. Goodall's porch, wondering what to do. If she went home, she could phone to find out what the woman wanted. She could say she had a stomachache. That wouldn't be a lie. And at home, she'd be safe.

Safe from what? She had liked Mrs. Goodall from the first day. She wasn't like everybody else. Come to think of it, she wasn't like anybody else. That's what made her interesting. And, no matter what Tiffany said, Mrs. Goodall was not a witch. This was her chance to tell her neighbor what she had seen. And she could meet the rest of the cats.

O.C., F.C., C.C., L.C. Such strange names for cats. Like people's initials. Suppose they *were* people's initials. Suppose Tiffany was right.

B.C., Beth thought. *Beth Carew.* Or, she imagined Mrs. Goodall's tinkling voice saying, "Best Cat."

The doorknob rattled.

Beth spun and fled down the stairs.

Mrs. Goodall said, "Why Beth Carew! How nice. Do come in," as if Beth were at the door instead of halfway across the lawn.

Beth took a deep breath and swallowed hard. Turning slowly, she said, "My mother said you wanted to see me?"

"I did?" Mrs. Goodall's face was pinched in thought. "Oh, yes, dear. I did. So many strange things go on in my house I sometimes forget what I'm about. Come in, dear. Come in," she said and disappeared inside.

Beth hung back. If she thought it was like entering another world to cross that hedge, what would it be like to step inside that house?

Mrs. Goodall's head popped out around the door.

"Hurry, dear," she said urgently, "or the cats will get out."

Beth glanced back over her shoulder. She looked hard at the grass, the trees, the sky, perhaps for the last time as a . . . girl! She wondered if cats could distinguish color. And then she followed Mrs. Goodall into the house.

Chapter Five

Mrs. Goodall was gone. It was as if the house had swallowed her. Alone in the dark, musty hall, Beth struggled for her breath.

Deep in the shadows opposite her, a door creaked. A figure in a long robe appeared.

In her head, Beth shouted, "Mrs. Goodall!" What came out was a terrified whisper.

The figure took two steps and stopped, still wrapped in shadow. Beth inched against the door, fumbling for the knob. "Mrs. Goodall?"

"Yes?" Mrs. Goodall appeared at the arched doorway on the right. Wrapped around her neck like a scarf was a spotted cat. "What's the matter, Beth dear? You look as if you'd seen a ghost."

Didn't the woman see it? Beth opened her mouth, but no words came. The figure was on the move again. He held a telephone receiver against the folds of the robe.

"Sibyl," he said urgently. "Quick. Tell me who is it."

"Beth Carew from next door," Mrs. Goodall answered.

He shook his head. "No. No." He wagged the telephone receiver in the air.

"On the phone? It's Imogene, dear. Don't you remember? You called her to make arrangements about our trip."

"No! *I!* Who am *I!* She asked 'Who is it?' and I can't remember!"

"Why, Avery Goodall!"

"That's it! Thank you." Into the phone he said, "Imogene? It's Avery. Avery Goodall!"

So this was Mr. Goodall. Beth was so relieved she almost giggled.

Mrs. Goodall sighed. "Poor Avery," she said, leading Beth into the living room. "He gets worse all the time. Sit down, dear."

The room was arranged so strangely that Beth didn't know where to sit. A low platform fronted the marble fireplace. On top, a high-backed red velvet chair rested like a throne. Facing the platform was a short row of theatre seats. A fragile-looking settee, an ornately carved coffee table, and two needlepoint chairs were bunched in a far corner.

Mrs. Goodall sat on the settee. The spotted cat slid into her lap.

The chair Beth eased into creaked under her. She sat very still, wishing she had chosen a sturdy theatre seat.

"You see, Avery always wanted to act. Unfortunately, it never quite worked out," Mrs. Goodall explained. "Now that he's retired, he plays so many parts he sometimes forgets who he really is."

"Doesn't everyone?" Mr. Goodall swept into the room and mounted the platform. "'All the world's a stage'" after all 'and all the men and women merely players.'" Lowering himself into the red velvet chair, he arranged his white robe in graceful folds about his sandals. With his white hair combed forward to form a kind of cap, he looked like a drawing in a history book.

19

"That may be so, Avery," Mrs. Goodall said, "but you have no idea how difficult it is talking to a person when you're never certain who that person is." To Beth she added, "It doesn't seem fitting somehow to ask a king to take out the garbage or let in the cat, for example."

"'Oh, what a rogue and *peasant slave* am I!'" Each of Mr. Goodall's words hung in the air for an instant before the next pushed it aside.

"Now, Avery." Mrs. Goodall leaned in. "He's angry with me for sending him out in the rain after F.C."

"Last night?" Beth asked. "In the storm? Then you're the one I saw!"

Mr. Goodall rose slowly. "'What, has this thing appeared again tonight?'" He descended the platform. "'Horatio says 'tis but our fantasy.'" Leaning forward, he plunged out of the room.

"Shakespeare," Mrs. Goodall said. "It's much easier to live with than all those Greeks. When Avery's doing them, he wears such dreadful masks."

The face in the window. The figure on the lawn. Mr. Goodall playing his roles. Beth laughed. It all seemed so obvious when you knew the answer.

Mrs. Goodall looked puzzled. After Beth explained, she said, "My heavens! How frightened you must have been."

"A little," Beth admitted. She surprised herself by adding, "But it was exciting. And now that it's all over, I think I'm going to miss it."

Mrs. Goodall nodded. "Yes, I can understand that." She leaned toward Beth as if she were about to share a confidence. "I'm a great fan of horror movies, you know. It's so delicious to be frightened—to feel your heart pounding and your blood rushing—when there's no real danger."

A tiger cat bounced toward them. When he saw Beth, his tail stiffened like a fire hose and the hair stood straight on the back of his neck.

Mrs. Goodall reached for him. "Here is someone who is always frightened."

"F.C.?"

"Yes. Wouldn't you know he'd be a tiger?"

"Where are the others?" Beth asked.

"Oh, my dear! I'm getting as forgetful as Avery. It's because of the cats I wanted to see you. I want you to meet them. It is very important that you like them and that they like you."

Now, it was Beth's turn to look puzzled.

Chapter Six

Beth burst into the kitchen. "Mom! Mom! Guess what?"

Her mother was sitting cross-legged on the floor, eyes closed, hands resting on her thighs, palms upward. Sometimes, she stood on her head. Meditating—withdrawn into her Self where she said all the answers were.

Exploding with excitement, Beth waited impatiently for her mother to come back to the world.

Mrs. Carew opened her eyes and smiled. "Babe! Hi."

"Find any answers?" Beth asked.

Mrs. Carew unwound and got to her feet. "Lately, I'm having trouble with the questions." She reached into the dishwasher for some potatoes. Since Mr. Carew couldn't repair it, she used it as a vegetable bin.

"I found some," Beth said. "And I got a job besides!"

The front doorbell rang.

"Oh, that's the man about jacking up the house," Mrs. Carew said. "If the babies wake up before I've finished with him, will you get them up?"

Beth nodded. Compared to getting people's attention around here, taking care of the cats, as Mrs. Goodall had asked her to do, would be no job at all.

Upstairs, a baby cried.

Not only was there no time to tell about her job in this

house, there was no time to think about it either. "Okay. I'm coming. I'm coming."

Beth had just brought Katie and John down when her mother led the man into the kitchen.

Mr. Owens ignored the introduction to the children and scrutinized the kitchen with narrow eyes.

"The floor is the worst right here," Mrs. Carew said. "It feels spongy. And everything seems to slope toward the middle of the house. I can set the vacuum near the sink and meet it in the dining room."

The man nodded. He tapped the walls and took out a level. Mumbling to himself, he laid it on the window sills, above the pantry door, and on the floor. "Floor's worst right here," he said. "Everything slopes toward the middle."

Beth and her mother exchanged amused glances. All that work to find out something they already knew!

Her mother took him down to the basement and up to the bedrooms. Beth could hear him tapping and bouncing all over the house.

At the front door, he said, "Cure's worse than the disease, missus."

"I thought we could disguise the sags," Mrs. Carew said, "but my husband thinks we should replace the old wooden posts in the basement with steel and put in a new beam under the kitchen."

Mr. Owens shook his head.

"You don't think we should do it?"

Mr. Owens snorted. "Cure's worse than the disease, missus."

* * *

23

"Owens didn't give you an estimate?" Mr. Carew asked at dinner.

"More like a diagnosis," Mrs. Carew answered.

Katie burped. "I hab gas-o-leen," she announced. When everyone laughed, she drew her head into her shoulders like a bird.

Beth seized the chance to get into the conversation. "I have something to tell you. The Goodalls are going on vacation and—"

The doorbell rang.

"It is impossible for a person to talk in this house!" Beth stormed out of the kitchen.

When she saw Paul Kallin, his back to the screen door, she became quiet—at least on the outside. On the inside, everything boiled and bubbled. *He's come to see me,* she thought.

"Hi," she said, biting back his name.

"Hi. My name's Kallin from down the street."

Hope plunged inside Beth. He hadn't come to see her at all. His face was too tight and serious.

"Is your father home?"

"He's eating dinner," she said.

"Oh," he said.

Then nobody said anything.

Mr. Carew came up beside her. "Who is it, Beth?"

The boy brightened. "Hi. My name's Kallin from down the street. Do you need your grass cut?"

Mr. Carew opened his mouth to speak.

"I have my own equipment," Paul hastened to add, "and my rates are reasonable."

"What about experience?" Mr. Carew asked.

Beth cringed. Was her father going to put him through a third degree?

"Oh, yes, sir. I've had lots of experience. This is my third summer."

"You're lucky. This is my first lawn," Mr. Carew said lightly, "and I enjoy cutting it myself."

"You do?" Paul looked surprised and puzzled. Then he smiled slowly. "But," he looked at the name on the mailbox, "Mr. Carew, you shouldn't trust such a magnificent lawn to someone who doesn't know what he's doing."

Mr. Carew laughed. "If you cut grass as well as you sell, you must be good. I'll tell you what: leave your card, and later on this summer when I'm busy working on the inside of the house, I'll give you a call."

The boy was unruffled. He whipped out a piece of paper, laid it on the porch rail, and took out a pen.

"Here you are, sir. My card." It read: *CALL PAUL*. In the corner under his telephone number, he had sketched a lawn mower and a patch of tall grass.

After the babies were in bed, Beth decided to give it one last try. She found her parents in the kitchen. Her father was thumbing through the telephone book for the numbers of people who jacked up houses, and her mother was drinking tea.

"Can you listen a minute?" she asked. "I have something I've been trying to tell you."

They both looked at her. Directly. It was a new sensation, like going barefoot for the first time after a long winter. Enjoying it, she settled into a chair. "All this attention," she said. "I can't believe it."

25

"What did you want to tell us, Babe?" her mother asked.

"The Goodalls are going on vacation and Mrs. Goodall asked me to take care of the cats while they're away and she's even going to pay me!" It was all out. Finally!

"Cats?" her father said. "With an *S?* Not in *this* house!"

"No, not here. In their own house. I'm to go over there twice a day and—"

"Alone?" Mrs. Carew interrupted. "In that big house alone? I'm not so sure I like that idea, Beth."

Beth groaned. First they pay absolutely no attention, she thought, and then they pay too much! "That Mr. Owens certainly knew what he was talking about," she said. "The cure *is* worse than the disease."

Chapter Seven

It took persuading, but her parents finally said Beth could cat sit. She would have been in a mess if they hadn't, since the Goodalls had left at five—unless they forgot they were going!

Beth hadn't thought of it before, but she realized now it was a good thing the babies had been born. Otherwise, her parents would have gone on treating her like a baby all her life. She might have lost some of their attention to the twins, but she had to admit she had gained a certain freedom.

She took her jacks and sat on the front steps. Across the street, Tiffany skipped. Somewhere, someone was barbecuing. A lawn mower droned. A dog barked.

Under the porch light, the jacks challenged her with long, confusing shadows. Beth was up to double-downs when Paul Kallin biked past with a group of friends. Then she scraped her knuckles and missed. She shrank into the shadows so they wouldn't see her sitting alone on her own front porch playing jacks.

What would she do, she wondered, without the cats to look forward to? One thing was certain: if she ever had children, she'd never move them in summer. It was never easy to make friends, but in summer, it was impossible.

Tiffany wandered up and sat beside her. "Want to go for a walk, Beth?"

"Are you sure your mother'll let you, Tiffany? It's getting dark."

"I already asked her. She said if you went and we didn't go far."

Beth dropped the jacks into her jeans' pocket. "I'm going for a walk," she called through the screen.

"Don't go far," her mother answered.

The corner streetlight came on as they approached. Insects and dust swirled in the beam of light. Beth stood on the curb tossing her red jacks' ball while Tiffany blew a dandelion into a shower of seeds.

"Which way, Tiffany?"

"Not that way!" Tiffany pointed at the Goodalls'.

Beth shrugged and headed away from the house on the corner. At the alley, she stopped short. Huddled under the next streetlight were the boys and girls who had biked past a few minutes before.

Abruptly, Beth started back.

Tiffany ran to catch up. "Where're we going?"

"It's this way or nothing, Tiffany."

Tiffany edged nearer. "All right. But if anything happens, Beth Carew, remember, I told you."

"There's nothing to be afraid of, Tiffany. The Goodalls aren't even home. It's just a house." Beth almost wished that weren't true. How much more exciting it would have been if Mrs. Goodall were a witch! If someone were imprisoned in the attic, or if the cats were not cats at all, but people under a spell, then she and Tiffany might have something to worry about. But now, with the mystery

28

solved, it was only a dark, silent house like hundreds of other houses.

"Let's go back," Tiffany whispered urgently.

Beth tugged her on. "Don't be a big baby, Tiffany. We're almost past."

Suddenly, in a back window, a light flashed on!

Chapter Eight

Tiffany screamed and took off like a rocket. Beth stared at the light for a few seconds. Then she streaked after Tiffany.

"Tiffany, wait!" she called. "Come back! Tiffanne-eee!"

She had to catch her. Little girls with big mouths couldn't be trusted to tell what they saw. By the time Mrs. Tanner heard the story, it wouldn't be one light in one window. The entire house would be ablaze, and shadowy figures would move in every window. Mrs. Tanner would rush over to the Carews. Someone would call the police. They would cart the cats off to a kennel. And Beth's cat sitting would be over before it began.

Out of her side vision, Beth saw a flash of movement. She leaped a low row of mulberry bushes into a garden and crouched there, listening. There was a rustling sound beside the house. Beth crept toward the house.

"Tiffany, it's me. I know you're there. Come on, I'll take you home."

"I am home, little girl. And that's where you should be!" The voice was deep and scratchy. Its owner, a large, dark shape, loomed closer, pointing something directly at her.

Beth took a running jump, skimmed the bushes, lost

her balance, and landed on all fours. She heard a sputtering behind her and felt a fine spray of water. She pushed herself up and ran. Halfway down the block, she doubled over. Her side hurt and her head throbbed. She sank to the parkway and fell back, gasping for breath. *A hose nozzle*, she thought. It was only a hose nozzle! She laughed, doubling up with the pain in her side.

Walking the rest of the way around the block, she tried to decide whether to mention the light in the Goodalls' window to her parents. She'd rather they heard it from her than from Mrs. Tanner, and they'd know from the look of her that something had happened. But if they knew, they might change their minds about letting her cat sit. That was a chance she didn't want to take.

She swept back the strands of hair that clung to her face like wet string, tucked in her shirt, and smoothed her jeans. There was a ragged tear in one knee and the point of a jack poked through a hole in her pocket.

"Psssttt! Beth."

Beth stopped short. "Who is it?" she said, peering into the darkness. "Who's there?"

Tiffany popped out from behind a tree. "Where were you?" she asked, taking hold of Beth's hand. "I've been waiting forever." Her eyes were wide with fear, and her body was trembling.

"You're the one who ran off," Beth said. "Did you go home?"

Tiffany shook her head.

Beth was relieved. Maybe she could talk Tiffany into forgetting what had happened. "Tiffany, maybe it would be better if we just forgot about the light. Okay? What I mean is there's probably a very simple explanation." Beth paused, trying to think of one. When she couldn't, she said, "Anyway, there's no sense telling your mother. You know that she'd just get all upset."

"Tell my mother! Not for a million trillion dollars."

Beth was surprised. "You're not going to tell your mother?"

Tiffany shook her head slowly. "Not my mother. Not anybody! You think I want that old Mrs. Goodall to find out and turn me into a cat or something?"

Beth's laugh was uneasy. Earlier today she had been thinking the very same ridiculous thoughts. "Oh, Tiffany, you know Mrs. Goodall isn't home."

"Witches don't have to be *home*," Tiffany said. She skipped across the street and disappeared around the side of her house.

Ahead, Beth's father moved the sprinkler across the front lawn. Cutting into the driveway, Beth quickened her pace. "Hi, Daddy," she called as she streaked past him. Mr. Carew waved without looking up. He hadn't noticed how awful she looked. Now if she could quickly sneak up to her room without her mother seeing her.

"I'm home," Beth called. She bounded up the stairs to her room, closed the door, and backslid to the floor. She'd made it. No one need ever know about the light in the window, and tomorrow she could begin her cat sitting without interference.

Unless someone was in that house! What if a burglar had turned on that light? Tomorrow, she'd find the house ransacked. How would she explain that to Mrs. Goodall? Whoever it was might still be there in the morning. In that case, Beth might not have the chance to explain anything to anyone ever again.

There was no getting away from it. She had to tell her parents about the light.

Sighing, Beth started down to the living room.

Chapter Nine

Beth's hand trembled as she tried to fit the Goodalls' back door key into the lock.

"Nothing to worry about," her father had assured her last night. "The light is probably connected to a timer set to go on for a few hours each night."

Beth wanted to believe him. He had investigated and found nothing amiss, but he hadn't gone into the house.

"I don't like nosing around in people's houses uninvited when it isn't necessary," he had explained. "Especially in houses with *five* cats."

The key connected. Beth slipped in and found Cat standing guard. He was a tabby, large and graceful—a no-nonsense cat with a no-nonsense name. He seemed so sure of himself that Beth soon forgot her apprehension.

She knelt on the kitchen floor to greet him, but he would have none of it. He circled her warily, the tip of his tail flicking. Finally, he went to the basement stairs and meowed. Three other cats bounded up the stairs and erupted into the kitchen.

Fraidy hunched his back and arched his tail like a Halloween cat cutout.

Beth laughed. "You should have been black like O.C."

O.C. cocked his head at the sound of his name. He wove between Beth's ankles, purring a greeting.

Copy, the spotted one, leaped to the table and licked the cat faces on the cat food cans.

Finally, Last Cat, a blue point Siamese, made a slow, dignified entrance. She sat apart from the others, staring through Beth with fixed blue eyes. She was the most beautiful and seemed to know it.

"Hello, L.C.," Beth said to her.

L.C. said, "Hi-ii."

Beth was astonished. "Would you mind repeating that?"

The cat gave it some thought, then washed her face instead.

While Beth opened their food, the cats, except L.C. who was too busy washing for breakfast, wandered around the kitchen, weaving in and out like dancers. They scampered over to the dishes Beth set on the floor.

While they ate, Beth looked around the kitchen. There was no staircase here. Otherwise, the Goodalls' kitchen was much like her own with an ordinary shelved room for the storage of food, and a butler's pantry with cabinets for china and silver, and a service counter. Beth poked behind doors, searching for the light she had seen last night. The swinging door to the butler's pantry was ajar, stuck on a rise in the floor. Behind it, Beth found a black coach-side light. *It was still on!*

"Maybe the timer's not working," she told herself. She looked everywhere in the small room, but there was no timer.

"Just because you don't know the explanation, doesn't mean there isn't one," she heard her father saying.

"Maybe the switch . . ." She flipped it. The light went out. Again. The light went on. It was working, but something about it seemed strange.

The cats surrounded her. C.C. leaped to the window over the service counter and batted the shade cord between her paws. L.C. took possession of the high stool where she could look down on the others. Tense as a snake about to strike, F.C. curled up under the stool. Cat and O.C. circled Beth in opposite directions.

"You don't belong in here," Beth scolded. "Come on. Out." Shooing them into the kitchen, she turned out the light and pulled the door shut behind her. With C.C. around her neck and O.C. in her arms, she herded them downstairs. Halfway down, O.C. leaped to the tiled basement floor and streaked up to the back door where he waited with Cat to be let out. The others had the freedom of the basement and the kitchen, but were not allowed outside the house. C.C. took a swipe at a sheet hanging over a line. She lost her balance and toppled from Beth's shoulder, landing solidly on all fours.

Back in the kitchen, Beth wondered what to do about the remaining cat food. Mrs. Goodall hadn't said, and Beth had never fed a cat before. Knowing something of their habits, she imagined they were nibblers. But the food was moist and the day was hot. Better they should be a little hungry, she decided, than sick from spoiled food.

She looked around for something to empty the dishes into. A bag leaned against the wall near the back door. It contained an empty milk carton, tea bags, and some chop bones. Beth smiled. His majesty Mr. Goodall had forgotten to take out the garbage. She scraped and washed the bowls, let Cat and O.C. out, dropped the bag in the garbage can outside the door, and started for home.

Mr. Goodall's forgetfulness! That was it! The Goodalls

must have returned to the house last night for something they had forgotten. One of them probably snapped on the light as she and Tiffany passed by, forgetting to switch it off again.

That evening, when Beth returned to care for the cats, she checked the light. It was off.

She went to bed pleased with herself for having found the answer. Now, if she knew what it was about the light switch that seemed odd. She fell into a restless sleep.

Instantly, she was feeling her way along a dark, endless corridor. Ahead, lights flashed on, going dark before she could reach them. Cats jumped at her, claws bared, eyes shining red. And in the distance, a piercing siren sounded. The sound grew louder!

In a cold sweat, Beth sprang up, her eyes wide with terror. It wasn't a siren! It wasn't part of her dream! It was the spine-chilling wail of something alive!

Her parents' bedroom door flew open. Her father raced across the landing.

"What's that noise?" Beth croaked.

Her father dashed down the stairs, with Mrs. Carew and Beth at his heels. He shined his flashlight out of the window beside the front door.

"It's not out there, Frank," Mrs. Carew said at his elbow. "It's coming from," she looked around helplessly, "the side of the house I think."

Beth could feel the sound shooting through her like a current through a wire. "It's everywhere," she said.

Mr. Carew flashed the light across the lawn.

"Maybe it's cats," her mother said.

Beth had heard cats in the night. She knew the hissing and the spitting, and the sound like babies crying. This

37

was not like that. This was like nothing she had ever heard—a high-pitched wail with a trill in it. "It's not cats," she said, teeth chattering.

Her father flicked off the light and crossed to the door. "Frank! You're not going out there!"

"Daddy! Don't open the door. Please, Daddy. Don't!"

"Will you two keep still!" He unlocked the door. Slowly, quietly, he eased it open.

The wailing seemed to grow, filling the room, bouncing off the walls like sonar.

Beth's stomach knotted and her knees shook. She opened her mouth to speak, but the words never got past the lump in her throat.

Mr. Carew beamed light through the screen. Suddenly, just when Beth thought she couldn't bear it another second, the sound stopped.

For several seconds, no one moved. The silence was more terrifying than the sound had been.

At last, Mr. Carew went out to the porch. "Nothing out here." He came in and locked the door.

At the window, Beth saw something move. "There it is!" A mound of blackness limped across the lawn. By the time her father looked, it was gone.

"To bed," he said, putting an arm around her shoulders. "Whatever it was is gone now." He put his other arm around her mother and the three of them went upstairs.

"I'm surprised the babies didn't wake up," Mrs. Carew said on her way in to check them.

"Maybe they did. Who could've heard them with that racket? I've never heard anything like it. I'm still shaking."

38

Beth was astonished. He had seemed so cool. "You too?" she said at the door to her room.

He kissed her forehead. "Me too."

It seemed like hours before Beth felt drowsy. She was beginning to think she might never sleep again, when she drifted off.

Far away across the hedge, something crashed and clattered.

Chapter Ten

At breakfast, Beth asked her mother, "You didn't hear anything else last night, did you, after we went to bed?"

"No. Why?"

"No reason," Beth said. "I just wondered." No sense mentioning the crash. She might have dreamed it, though she doubted it. She felt it and that dreadful wailing were somehow related. Her mother would worry if she knew, and she might forbid Beth to go into the Goodalls' alone.

"It's settled," Mr. Carew said as he hung up the phone. "Mr. Fink will be here first thing tomorrow morning."

Mrs. Carew looked doubtful. "You're sure he knows what he's doing?"

"He's moved houses for thirty years," Mr. Carew said.

Mrs. Carew smiled. "But we don't want the house moved, Frank—just straightened a bit."

Beth excused herself and left for the Goodalls'. She went the front way, following the path taken by whatever it was she had seen last night. She hoped to find broken twigs, a patch of rooted-up grass, or any clue to the identity of the noisemakers. There was nothing.

She circled the house, checking to see if anything metal had fallen. That would explain the clatter. The gutters were securely in place and the garbage can lids, though one was slightly awry, were where they belonged. Could the crash have come from inside the house?

Beth slipped in the back door cautiously, prepared for anything. The house was unnaturally quiet. Maybe the cats had knocked something over last night and were skulking guiltily in the basement.

"Cat!" Beth called. "O.C.?"

A terrifying squall startled her. There was no mistaking the sound of cats. But what was the matter with them? She stood absolutely still, afraid even to breathe. They knew she was here. Why didn't they come bounding into the kitchen? They would do that unless they couldn't! Was someone down there, holding them prisoner? Were they trying to warn her?

She had to do something! She edged to the broom cupboard and eased the door open—very slowly. The broomstick slipped from her sweating hand. She caught it before it hit the floor. Grasping it firmly in both hands, she held it to her shoulder like a bat. Then she crossed to the basement door. There was no human sound. She pressed against the wall and eased onto the first step.

Whoever it was could be anywhere in the shadows below. He could reach out and grab her ankles. He could rush up the stairs and pin her arms before she could swing the broom. He could wait until she was down there and come at her from behind. She groped for the light switch along the wall beside her. She would expose herself with the light, but that was a chance she'd have to take. She flicked it and plunged downward, holding the broom like a shield.

Suddenly, she dropped the broom and sank to the bottom step, shaking with laughter. There in the middle of the floor the sheet rose and shifted like a snowdrift in the wind. Along the edge, five cat tails twitched.

When she had caught her breath, Beth untangled sheet from cats and cats from cats. Fraidy scratched her arm. Copy went limp on the cool floor. O.C. rubbed himself against her legs appreciatively. Cat bounded up to the kitchen. And L.C. washed herself carefully, scolding Beth now and then as though it were her fault the sheet had fallen off the clothesline.

She petted and soothed them until everyone, herself included, was calm enough to go upstairs for breakfast.

In the kitchen, Beth stepped over the cats to the sink. "You'll have to wait for your breakfast until I wash this scratch."

Creak.

She whirled.

The pantry door swung open.

There *was* someone here! Beth gripped the edge of the sink, waiting. The clock ticked. The refrigerator whirred. Cat ambled into the pantry. Beth gasped. C.C. jumped to the sink and gave her a gentle tap on the cheek, her yellow-green eyes shining with concern. Cat returned to the pantry door where he sat looking at Beth as if to say, "You see. There's nothing."

Relief poured through her. She reached gratefully for Cat, but he squirmed loose and strode off. Beth laughed and shut the pantry door without a glance inside.

She tried to hurry the cats through breakfast. Cat picked at the food as if he were doing her a favor to eat it at all. The others turned up their noses. When Beth was certain they wouldn't eat, she cleaned the dishes.

42

"That'll teach you to tangle with a sheet," she said. "You're so upset you've lost your appetites."

She had promised Mrs. Goodall she'd get the mail, but the thought of walking through the house alone after what she'd been through already this morning made her stomach knot, so she took the cats with her. A mistake. The minute they were out of the kitchen, they scattered.

The heavy drapes kept out the sun so that the house was dark even at this time of morning. Beth followed a dusty shaft of sunlight slanting through a hall window as though it were the light at the end of a tunnel. She couldn't help but feel she was living last night's dream.

Outside the front door, she nearly tripped over a large crate addressed to the Goodalls. She tried unsuccessfully to lift it. Lemons. What would anyone want with an entire crate full of lemons? Even the fragrance of them gave her a twinge at the back of her jaw.

As she tugged the crate into the hall, Copy Cat pounced out of the shadows and landed on her shoulder, claws digging.

"Don't do that," Beth scolded. "There're enough surprises in this house as it is."

C.C. purred and wrapped herself around Beth's neck.

"Let's round up the others," Beth said to her.

O.C. did a tightrope act down the banister when Beth called. F.C. was clinging to a drape. L.C. was right where Beth had expected—in the living room, sitting sphinx-like in the center of the red velvet chair. Cat was at the back door waiting to be let out.

At home, her mother was crawling around the kitchen floor.

"New exercise?" Beth joked.

Mrs. Carew sat back on her heels and brushed the hair from her eyes. "The oven. I opened the door to check the cake and it fell apart in my hands."

The oven door was in two parts like upper and lower jaws with the insulation lolling to one side like a fuzzy tongue. Beth helped her mother gather the nuts and bolts and started for her room.

"Oh, Beth," Mrs. Carew said, "there's some mail for you on the bookcase in the living room."

It was a postcard from Mrs. Goodall.

We got away on time, and—wonder of wonders— we didn't have to return for a thing. Avery did forget to take out the garbage. I'm sure you've discovered that by now. If you need us, we're at Imogene's.

The words, *we didn't have to return for a thing,* jumped out at Beth. Then who had turned on the light? Someone was in the house on the corner.

"I need you all right, Mrs. Goodall," she said, examining the postcard. True to form, the woman had forgotten to include Imogene's address. There was no last name, and the postmark was smeared.

Chapter Eleven

The cats wouldn't eat. This morning, even Cat turned up his nose at the full dish Beth set before him.

Beth stroked him, saying, "You're angry because I was late, is that it?" She had stayed home to watch Mr. Fink. Before she left, he had propped the house with wooden posts and was placing the jack screws. She was anxious to see what happened when he began turning the giant screws that would raise and level the floors.

But the way things were going, she'd never get home. First, she had found the butler's pantry door ajar and the light on. After Mrs. Goodall's postcard, she had almost expected that. Nonetheless, it was unsettling. And now the cats roamed the kitchen aimlessly, refusing to eat, hunching and stretching as though they were made of springs.

Watching them made Beth jumpy and thirsty. It was so hot. Her long hair scratched her neck like wool, and her blouse was glued to her back. She stepped over the cats to the sink for a drink.

Behind her, the pantry door creaked open.

Beth's stomach dropped. She crossed to the pantry slowly, trying to keep calm. She paused, sniffing. Lemons! She fumbled for the light. The cats crowded into the pantry. Beth found the chain and pulled. There was the same crate of lemons she had left in the hall.

C.C. ambled along a shelf. "Get down from there before you knock—" Too late. Beth lunged to catch the toppling boxes and tripped over the lemon crate. The boxes fell around her with a series of dull thuds. The cats scrambled out. Beth gathered the boxes, murmuring, "How did I get into this?"

She left the light on and the door open and sank into a chair facing the pantry. She couldn't afford to turn her back on that door again.

Think, she commanded herself. *How did that crate get in there? And why does that door keep opening?* If someone were in the house, as she suspected, that would explain the lemons. But not the door. No one, however quick, could open that door and get away without being seen.

Beth swept her hair up off her neck. It was too hot to think. It was too hot to do anything.

C.C. leaped to the table beside her. "All right, Miss Troublemaker, did you move the lemons?" Beth asked, reaching for her.

C.C. swatted Beth's hand, dived off the table, and landed beside Fraidy. Yowling, F.C. streaked into the butler's pantry and disappeared.

"Fraidy! You come back here!" Beth ran after him.

The others ran after her.

"F.C.!" she called as she groped through the dark house. "Don't be afraid." That was asking a lot when her own heart was beating double-time.

If someone were in the house, where would he be? Something moved behind her. She whirled and stumbled

46

over a cat! Her ankle twisted and gave way. She fell down, tears of pain and frustration filling her eyes. Something cool and moist brushed her cheek. "Go away, you stupid cat!" she cried. There was a soft meow, followed by the padded sound of running cat feet.

At that moment, Beth hated every last cat! She rubbed her throbbing ankle. I can't stay here like a sitting duck, she thought. She made a circle with her ankle. It hurt, but it wasn't broken. She pulled herself up and tested her ankle.

She limped to the front hall. A pair of shining eyes peered down at her from the staircase. Coaxing F.C. with soft words, she ascended slowly, wincing at every step. He was within reach. If she missed and he streaked upstairs, she would have to go after him. She wouldn't let herself think about what might be up there.

"Got you!" she said with her hands on him.

But the cat slid through her fingers and bounded up the stairs. Beth pitched forward and hit her nose against a stair. Her eyes stung with tears. She lay there moaning. Copy climbed on her back. O.C. licked her face. Beth shook them off angrily and reached for the banister.

In the gloomy first floor landing, she froze. All those rooms and cupboards and corners. Hiding places.

Her voice thick with fear, Beth called, "I know you're here!" She counted to ten. All was silent. "You might as well come out!"

A door swung shut.

Before she realized what she was doing, Beth jerked it open. A steep flight of stairs led into the attic. "So you're up there, are you?" Pressed against the wall, she inched upward. She had started this game of *come out, come out, wherever you are;* now she had to finish it.

Something moved above.

Beth strained to see. "Fraidy?"

She edged forward, heart pounding. "Fraidy! Come down here."

Something hurtled down, knocking her against the wall. It dropped over her head and slipped down her shoulders. Beth flailed her arms, fighting to get loose. Her breath exploded as a round hardness dashed against her. "Fraidy!" The cat clung, its claws sharp as thorns.

Beth fell back onto a step stroking the cat. His fur crawled under her hand. "It's all right. It's all right," she said. The robe that had entangled her lay in a heap at her feet. It was one of Mr. Goodall's costumes. Today, F.C. had been wearing it.

There was no one up here—at least no one to be frightened of. If someone had meant to harm her, he would have done so by now. "I guess I'm the fraidy cat," Beth said aloud. "Come on, let's put this robe back where it belongs." In the excitement, she had forgotten her ankle. Now it shot pain up her leg with every step.

The attic was filled with trunks and chests and pipe racks and the odor of moth balls. Beth thought she saw something move. She stood still. The movement stopped. It was only her hazy reflection in an old mirror. F.C. had such a fierce hold on her, she couldn't manage to get the robe on a hanger. She draped it over a rack and made a slow, painful descent. Someday, with Mr. Goodall's permission, she would like to come back up here.

Weak and dizzy from the heat and the pain, Beth rested on the landing. She thought she'd never make it.

F.C. meowed and squirmed in her arms. He was impatient to get moving.

"One step at a time," Beth murmured. "One step—"

Downstairs, a door slammed.

Beth tightened her hold on the cat.

Another door slammed.

She could *feel* the sound. She held her breath, waiting. Fraidy wriggled and broke loose. Beth held back a scream. She crept down, limping silently through the house.

Meowing sadly, F.C. scratched at the door to the kitchen. It was closed! She cracked it open slowly. F.C. scooted through. Beth waited the space of a few stabbing breaths. Then she thrust her head in, ready to swing the door shut on whoever was behind it.

Everything was in peaceful order. The lights in both pantries were out and the doors closed. L.C. washed herself on the window sill. C.C. toyed with a loose thread under a chair. Cat stared fixedly at nothing. F.C. went into the basement, and Beth assumed O.C. was there too. She called him, but he didn't respond. She was not going to look for him! It wouldn't hurt him to stay in one day.

She found a paper and pencil. Her hand shook as she wrote:

Who is in this house?
Please Answer.

She put the note in the center of the table and turned

to leave. Suddenly, Cat started violently as if he had seen something invisible to the human eye.

Beth added:

If you can!!!

to the note and left the house. Quickly.

Chapter Twelve

Looking concerned, Mrs. Carew asked, "What did you do to your ankle?" as Beth propped her foot on a chair.

"Twisted it." It sounded so ordinary here in her own kitchen. It was amazing how you could tell the facts without really telling the truth.

"You sit there," her mother said, "and I'll get an elastic bandage."

"Please don't," Beth said. "It'll be all right." Even the words *elastic bandage* sounded hot. "I'd feel like a mummy all wrapped up in one of those things."

"Well then, how about a nice cold glass of lemonade?"

Beth laughed. "Anything but lemonade! If I never see another lemon, it'll be too soon. You won't believe this, but the way I look all started with a crate full of lemons."

"Ice water?" her mother asked, pouring a tall glassful from the frosty pitcher.

Beth accepted the glass with grateful thanks, and held it to her flaming cheeks.

Her mother sat beside her. "Do you want to tell me what happened?"

Beth was trying to decide where to begin when her father trudged up from the basement. He had taken the morning off to watch Mr. Fink.

"He's ready to—Aahh-CHOO!" He darted a glance Beth's way.

It was the cat dander on her clothes. "I was just going," she said, and hobbled for her room.

As she stepped into her shorts, the house rumbled and shook. Standing on one foot, Beth looked up, expecting to see the walls collapsing. She tripped and collapsed herself. Today was definitely not her day.

"Beth? Are you all right?" her mother called.

"Fine," she answered, adding, "I'm the one that needs jacking up," under her breath.

She found her family in the living room. Katie and John huddled close to Mrs. Carew on the low radiator under the front windows. Mr. Carew paced the floor. "Here's a new crack." He traced the ragged line at the dining room arch with an index finger.

"Paint falling, Bessie," John said, his blue eyes stormy with fear.

The house shuddered. Loose plaster rattled between the walls. Suddenly, like a jagged lightning bolt, another crack appeared.

Silently, Beth joined the others on the radiator.

Mr. Fink lumbered into the room, his hair and overalls frosted gray with plaster dust. Nodding, he surveyed the damage.

"You're sure the house isn't going to come apart at the seams, Mr. Fink?" Mrs. Carew pretended to be joking, but it was obvious from the quiver in her voice she was more frightened than amused.

Mr. Fink placed and re-placed his level. Beth half expected him to say, "Cure's worse than the disease, missus." Instead, he said, "A few cracks," and shrugged as if it were nothing. A chunk of plaster hit him on the head, which, Beth suspected, was what her mother wanted to do.

"It is kind of scary," Beth said.

Mr. Fink smiled a slow, shy smile. "Scary? Naw. No different'n jacking up a car to change a tire."

"But a person's not in the car when it's jacked up," Beth said.

"Don't you worry, little lady. This here's a good, sound house." He tapped the wall. Paint chips flew in all directions.

He conferred with Mr. Carew and decided to give it another quarter-turn. The two of them went back downstairs.

"Beth!" Tiffany's voice drifted through the screen door.

"Hi, Tiffany." Beth opened the door, marvelling at Tiffany's appearance. Her crisp, white dress had not a wrinkle, and, even in this heat, not a single curl had sprung.

Tiffany stepped into the hall. "I came to tell you—"

The house trembled.

"What's *that?*"

"What's what?" Beth asked.

Something walked between the walls.

"That!"

"I don't hear anything, Tiffany."

Tiffany's eyes scanned the room. "Well, I just came to tell you that I'm leaving for my vacation," she called as she bolted down the steps.

"Poor Tiffany," Mrs. Carew said.

"I know," Beth answered, "but I couldn't resist it. She's such a scaredy-cat."

"Everyone's afraid of something, Beth."

"Tiffany's afraid of everything!" *The pot calling the kettle black,* Beth thought.

"I know she's a nuisance sometimes, but you just wait, you're going to miss her while she's away."

Shortly after noon, Mr. Fink and his helper left. They would return to begin the back part of the house first thing in the morning.

Mrs. Carew was relieved to see them go. "Now we can get back to normal," she said.

But Beth noticed that her mother moved carefully, taking soft steps as if she thought the slightest noise would bring the house down. And after the babies' nap, she was anxious to get them outside. Beth was drafted to take them for a walk.

"Take your time, Babe," Mrs. Carew said as she helped the twins out of the door. "There's a ball game at the park this afternoon. Maybe you'll see someone you know."

"Like who?" Beth mumbled.

Early in the summer Mrs. Carew had sent for all the park district schedules. Beth had looked them over (golf, baseball, crafts—the usual) and tossed them aside. She certainly wasn't going to go to any of those things alone! But her mother made periodic announcements of scheduled events. Beth was tempted to tell her to go herself if she was so interested.

The Tanners' lawn was lush and green and smelled newly mown. Their windows glittered golden in the late afternoon sun. Still, the house had a forlorn, abandoned look. Even if Tiffany hadn't told her they were leaving on vacation, Beth thought she would have known. Houses were like people. No matter how cheerful they appeared on the outside, if the inside were empty, it showed through.

Beth sighed. Though she hated to admit it, she missed Tiffany already. Six more weeks until school. This was the first time she could remember wishing the summer away.

She glanced up to see three bicycles approaching. Paul Kallin and two of his friends! She dropped down on the far side of the stroller and pretended to tie her sneaker.

Katie leaned over the side. "You fall, Bessie?"

Despite herself, Beth laughed. She could never be a secret agent with Katie for a sister.

It was nearly dark when she returned to the Goodalls'.

Though she hadn't let him out this morning, O.C. was sitting on the back step.

And the note was gone!

Chapter Thirteen

Beth lay awake long after her family was asleep. She went over and over the strange things that had happened, hoping to find some clue that would unravel the entire mystery of the house on the corner.

She began with the cats. Two mornings in a row they hadn't eaten. Yesterday, she had thought it was because of their upsetting tangle with the sheet. Today, no such thing had happened. And she had been late this morning. Yesterday she had not been. There were no common circumstances that could explain both times.

Another thing: who had been in the house while she was in the attic? And how did O.C. turn up in the back garden when she had not let him out?

Twice the light was on. Both times, she remembered now, the butler's pantry door had been ajar. And there was something curious about the switch. She had the feeling she knew what it was if she could only find the words. It was like meeting someone whose face was familiar but whose name she'd forgotten.

There was the pantry door. Even now, she could hear it creaking and smell the lemons inside.

The disappearance of the note.

Finally, that terrifying wail and the crash and clatter. Was the house haunted? Even Mrs. Goodall had remarked about the strange things that went on in her house. "A mind of its own," she had said. Ghosts could explain everything. Her father would tell her she was imagining things. "Look for a simple explanation," he would say.

A simple answer. There had to be one. But the more she thought about it, the more complicated it seemed. Nothing fitted with anything else. It was as if the pieces of several different puzzles were mixed together in the same box.

Beth sighed and slid down under her sheet. Her mobiles circled over her head. She felt the answers were there all right, like the mobiles—shapes in the darkness just out of reach.

Next morning, Cat's pink tongue circled his mouth when he saw her as if to say, "Good. You're here. Now we can eat."

O.C. rubbed himself against her legs.

L.C. said, "Hi-ii."

C.C. untied Beth's shoelaces.

Even F.C. seemed happy to see her. No bared claws or hunched back or hisses. And he allowed Beth to stroke him once or twice before he curled his tail under his body and slunk off.

Everything was so normal, in fact, Beth was willing to believe she had imagined everything. The house was spooky, after all, with its heavy draperies and dark wall coverings. And the Goodalls were unlike any neighbors Beth had ever known. To say nothing of the cats. It was no wonder superstitions had grown up around them over the centuries. Their independent natures and strange ways defied understanding. Under the circumstances, Beth concluded, it was easy to imagine all kinds of things.

Imagination. A nice simple answer. It could explain the crash she had heard the other night. After that other-worldly wailing on their lawn, she was jumpy enough to imagine anything. Perhaps the cats hadn't eaten because they weren't hungry. And O.C. could have got out through a basement window.

Deep in thought, Beth leaned back against the sink.

Slowly the pantry door swung open.

Beth moaned. "That puts me right back where I started!" No matter how she stretched it, imagination did not cover the door or the lemons or the light or the note.

What I need is help, she decided. She let Cat and O.C. out and went home, ready to tell her mother the whole baffling story regardless of the consequences.

But Mrs. Carew was crying.

"Mom? What's the matter?" Beth asked, knowing the answer. A network of cracks scarred the recently painted kitchen wall.

Mrs. Carew blew her nose and wiped her eyes. The house groaned. A bit of plaster fell at her feet. She took up a broom. Smiling wanly at Beth, she said, "I feel like Chicken Little."

So did Beth. Luck seemed to have turned against her. Her own house kept looking worse instead of better. The mystery became more complicated every day. And there was no one to share it with—not a single friend to show for the weeks she'd lived here. Things couldn't have been more dismal if the sky were falling.

Later, sunbathing in the garden Beth decided there was no way she could solve the mystery, so she wouldn't try. Maybe the Goodalls would return early. If not—well, nothing too serious had happened to her so far. If she spent as little time as possible in that evil house, maybe nothing would.

The black squirrel scampered toward her. A few feet away, he sat up to beg.

"I have nothing for you so go away and leave me alone," Beth snapped.

The squirrel stepped closer.

Beth hissed at him. He whirled and skittered up a tree. In a split second, she had probably undone all the progress she had made trying to tame him. So what? she thought. Taming all the squirrels in the world wouldn't make them anything but squirrels; only a person could be a friend. As crowded as it had been, she wished they had never left their city apartment.

She rolled to her stomach and idly picked at a clover patch. She broke off a leaf and counted the sections. Four! She sat up. A four-leaf clover! In her whole life she had found only one other. She rooted through the patch. There was another. And another. In all, she unearthed seven. Seven four-leaf clovers!

Her luck had to change. She jumped up and made for the house. She would see to it that it changed. Enough of this feeling sorry for herself.

Beth filled a glass with water and put in the clover leaves. "I found seven four-leaf clovers!" she told her mother.

Mrs. Carew thumbed through the paint and wallpaper section of a catalogue. "Maybe you could spare me some of your luck. I think I'm going to need it," she said, but the tears had dried and she was smiling.

Beth put the clovers on her dresser. She took out note-book paper and made a chart with two headings:

Unusual Happenings
Possible Solutions

By the time she had finished, it was clear that nothing, with the possible exception of the crash and clatter that one night, was imagined.

She could understand why her father made his work lists. Writing things down didn't get them done, but it did help to establish a starting point. Studying her own list, Beth decided to begin with the light in the butler's pantry. The switch, she felt, was some kind of clue, the only real clue she had.

That settled, she headed another sheet:

People I Know

Under that she wrote *Tiffany Tanner* in ink and *Paul Kallin* in pencil. Knowing someone's name and face was not enough to make him permanent.

Midway down the page she put: *What Have I Done to Make Friends?*

The answer—*NOTHING!!!*—was an accusation.

Chapter Fourteen

Click. Beth's bedroom light flashed on. *Click.* It went off. An ordinary switch. How was it different from the one next door? Beth tried it again.

"I'll never figure it out," she said. "Maybe the others . . ."

She went into all the upstairs rooms flipping switches. The babies' room was last. This switch was different from the others. It was silent. No click. Beth closed her eyes and imagined herself in the Goodalls' butler's pantry. She flipped the button up, down, up, down. It slid into place with very little pressure. It felt right. Familiar.

"That's it! Theirs is a silent switch." But she wasn't satisfied. "There's something else."

The landing had two switches. One controlled the upstairs light and the other, the light in the downstairs hall. Beth flipped each several times, chanting, "Up for on. Down for off. Up for on. Down for off."

She pushed the switches up one last time and slumped to the top step. "I'm getting nowhere!" she murmured.

Suddenly, both lights went off.

"Hey! What's going on up there?" Her father was in the front hall. He had turned the lights off from downstairs.

Beth jumped up to examine the switches. The positions

here were now reversed: *up* for off; *down* for on! That was it! The Goodalls' switch was not only silent, it was upside down!

"Thanks, Dad. You're a great help!" Beth said, nearly slamming into him as he came up and she went down.

He stepped aside. "If this's the way you treat a help, I'd sure hate to be a hindrance."

Beth was out of the door, heading for the Goodalls', when her mother called her back.

"Help the babies into their chairs, please, Beth," Mrs. Carew directed as she maneuvered the broiler pan out of the oven. The door, though put back together, did not open all the way.

Mr. Carew came up behind his wife. "Steak! What're we celebrating? Our straight floors?"

He bounced in the center of the linoleum. "Look at that! Solid."

A sprinkle of paint chips dropped to the counter like a silent snowfall.

"We are not celebrating anything." Mrs. Carew's voice was icy. "As long as the broiler in that ridiculous oven is on whether I want it on or not, I might as well use it. It's easier than trying to keep everything from getting scorched on the top."

Mr. Carew sat down at the table. "It's on the list, Mary. A new stove. Any kind you want."

"Oh, I know, Frank. Don't pay any attention to me. I've been so upset all day, I couldn't even stand on my head!"

Beth and her father laughed. The twins studied them quizzically for a few seconds. Then they too began to laugh.

After dinner, Mr. Carew asked, "Have you noticed a difference in the doors? Fink warned me they'd shift."

"The pantry," Mrs. Carew answered. "It sticks."

Mr. Carew checked it carefully. "It needs a little sanding. I'll do it tonight." He crossed to the basement door. "How about this one? Does it still stick?"

"Close it," Mrs. Carew directed, "and I'll show you."

He pushed it shut. "Seems to have eased up a bit."

"That is an understatement. Watch." She took a step toward the stove.

The door swung slowly open.

"It's contagious," Beth said, thinking of the Goodalls' pantry door. When her mother demonstrated a second time, something clicked in Beth's mind. Every time the pantry door had swung mysteriously open, she had been standing at the sink. Was that the answer then? A simple case of an old house with loose floorboards and ill-fitting doors?

Beth hurried through the dishes. Now that she had time to think about it, she knew the business with the light was only partially solved. Knowing how the switch was different did not explain how the light had come on in an empty house. Discouraging, except for her discovery about the door. She hoped that was one puzzle piece locked firmly into place.

She emptied the washing-up bowl and gave the sink a wipe with the cloth. "I'm going next door," she said, starting out.

"Not until you help your mother put the babies to bed," her father said.

Beth grumbled her way upstairs. When she came down again, her father was replacing the pantry door.

"And take out the garbage, please," he said.

Beth thought Mr. Goodall had the right idea. Maybe she too would be an actor and play only people too important to wash dishes and change babies and take out the garbage.

She went the front way to pick up the Goodalls' mail. She was not going to chance going through that house ever again. Crossing the lawn, she looked up at the house. The sky was a fiery backdrop. The house was spooky, all right, and old. It seemed to lean so far forward it would hardly have surprised her to see the roof slide off. Come to think of it, nothing about that house would surprise her anymore.

Nothing except . . . THE FACE THAT APPEARED SUDDENLY IN THE ATTIC WINDOW!

Chapter Fifteen

The enormous hollow eyes, the gaping mouth! Beth would never forget that face. She fought the urge to run. Someone or something was in the house that very minute. She had to go in. If she didn't, she would never know who or what! She ducked around the side of the house.

Her hands trembled as she fished the key from her jeans' pocket. Suppose it had seen her and was in the kitchen now, waiting? She dropped the key. It clinked against the garbage can and ricocheted onto the lawn. Beth poked the grass with her foot until she found it, but as she reached for it, she heard a noise just inside the door. Beth froze. The scratching noise grew louder. If *it* were there, it had seen her for certain. Yet there was nothing at the window in the back door.

As Beth moved to the door, the scratching stopped. She peered inside. Cat sidled up the stairs into the kitchen. What was he doing inside?

Hands shaking, Beth fumbled with the lock. But the door was open!

Four cats (F.C. was missing) milled about the kitchen as if they were waiting for something to happen. Beth stood in their midst, listening. The cats meowed. Her heart pounded. There was no other sound.

Could she have been mistaken? What she had seen was

one of Mr. Goodall's masks. She had assumed someone was behind it. Could it have been an empty mask? Perhaps it had not appeared suddenly as she had thought; perhaps it had been in the window all along and she had merely noticed it suddenly.

Shutting the cats in behind her, Beth crossed through the butler's pantry into the dining room. The house was deadly quiet. She sneaked into the front hall.

Could it have been F.C.? Perhaps he had got out somehow and made for the attic. Rummaging around up there, he had knocked over a mask. Yes, that was it. Well, he could come down when he was good and ready. Beth was not going after him.

Returning to the kitchen, she remembered the open back door. Maybe I left it open this morning, she thought. The way things had been going, she could easily have forgotten all about it. And Cat and O.C.? How had they got back into the house? An open window in the basement? She would have to check.

Beth prepared the cats' supper. She would check her theories about the pantry door and the light switch while they ate. That is, *if* they ate.

They did. Eagerly. Except C.C., who had disappeared.

"C.C.?" Beth called. "Where are you?" First F.C. and now C.C.—the case of the disappearing cats. She checked the butler's pantry. No spotted cat. She flipped the switch. Down for on. Up for off. It was upside down. Now if she knew what, if anything, that meant.

She glimpsed Copy under the kitchen table in mock battle with what looked like a ball of crumpled paper. Beth groaned. It's probably a piece of mail!

"Copy! Come here, you silly cat." Beth crawled in

66

after her. "That's a pretty kitty." As she reached for the cat, her hand froze at the sound of something overhead. She sat up and hit her head. The cats bounded toward her. "You pick the strangest times to play," she said, shaking them off. She backed out from under the table and sat on her heels, rubbing the bump on her head, and straining to hear.

Silence.

"There you go again," she said aloud. "It's nothing. The house creaking. Or F.C. rolling something around. That's all."

There it was again.

Footsteps!

Beth stood. Her knees felt like used rubber bands. Steadying herself against the table, she picked her way through the cats to the butler's pantry.

Thump. Thump.

Directly overhead!

The sound was like the echo of her own heartbeat. She cracked open the dining room door. Suddenly, it was wrenched from her hand. The cats rammed into it and scrambled through. Beth felt her way through the house, pausing every few steps to listen. Overhead, the sound stopped and started too. Like cat and mouse, Beth thought, her skin crawling. And *I'm the mouse!*

The thumping noise came louder and closer. Someone was coming down the stairs toward her. She withdrew into the shadows, mind racing. She was cornered. *Please don't let him see me,* she pleaded silently. Her heart hammered in her ears. The figure paused. *He knows I'm here!* She clapped her hand over her mouth to keep from screaming.

67

He descended slowly. Closer. Closer.

Beth's whole body tensed to scream. What escaped the cage of her fingers was a laugh!

"What are *you* doing here?"

Chapter Sixteen

It was Paul Kallin!

"I'm supposed to be here," Beth said. "Mrs. Goodall hired me to—"

"—take care of the cats," Paul finished. "I should have known!"

"What about you?" Beth asked him.

"Mr. Goodall hired me."

Good old Mr. Goodall, Beth thought, he must have forgotten to tell his wife. "That explains everything," she said.

"It sure does." Paul sank to a step. "Here I thought the cats weren't eating because they missed the Goodalls, and all the time you'd already fed them."

"Except when you beat me to it."

Paul nodded. "I came early one morning so I could go fishing."

"And the next morning," Beth put in, "I was late. Wait a minute! That day I went upstairs after F.C. and I heard a door slam down here. If you'd already been here . . . ?"

"I forgot to let the cats out so I came back, only Cat wouldn't go out. I was glad I came back though, because there were lights on and doors open all over." He laughed. "I thought I'd left it like that. I was beginning to think my mom was right She's always telling me I have a memory like a sieve."

"You? I thought it was me! Finding O.C. at the back door when I couldn't remember letting him out . . ."

"Well, I rode all over the neighborhood looking for him that night. When he turned up inside, I figured he'd gone in through a basement window or something."

"And you moved the lemons!"

"Yeah," he said. "I thought it was funny that the Goodalls would leave a crate like that in the hall."

Beth saw something move on the stairs behind Paul. "Don't look now," she said, "but we're being watched."

"Come on. The mystery's solved, remember?"

"No, really. I think it's F.C."

As Paul turned, the cat flashed past them.

"That stupid cat has caused me more trouble," Paul said. "I followed him up to the attic, but I couldn't find him in that jumble."

"You found the masks though, didn't you?"

Paul looked sheepish. "How'd you know?"

"I saw a mask in the window."

"Oh, I was behind it all right. It's like being on the inside of a baseball mitt."

Beth and Paul rounded up the cats and took them back to the kitchen.

"What I don't understand," Beth said, "is why you didn't answer my note."

"What note?"

"You mean you didn't see it?"

Paul shook his head.

C.C. was back under the table knocking the paper ball between her paws.

"Come to think of it, I have a pretty good idea what happened to it." Beth wrested the paper from Copy, who fled into the butler's pantry, and handed it to Paul.

"You weren't really scared, were you?" he asked as he read it.

"Me? Scared? Never! Faces in windows. Notes, cats, lemons disappearing. Doors opening by themselves. Happens every day."

"Doors opening?"

"Watch." Beth stepped to the sink and the pantry door creaked on its hinges.

Paul gave a low appreciative whistle. "How'd you do that?"

Beth smiled. "My secret . . . which I'll keep until you admit you were scared too."

"Why be scared? There had to be a simple explanation."

"That's what was so confusing. There wasn't a simple answer at all; there were several. And I kept thinking of the wrong things as clues. Take the light. I know now that you were in here the night the Goodalls left, but at the time—"

Paul's face went blank. "I wasn't here that night."

"Be serious," Beth said. "I saw your friends down the street waiting for you."

"The first time I came in was the morning after they left."

Beth started for the butler's pantry.

The light flashed on.

The color drained from Paul's face. "Who . . . who's in there?"

Beth thought she knew the answer. With the switch

and the partially open door, two more puzzle pieces had fallen into place. "Why don't you go and see? No reason to be scared," she teased. "There has to be a simple answer."

Paul squared his shoulders and went in. "There's no one here!"

"No one?"

"Only Copy Cat."

Copy sat on the counter washing her face. Beth snapped off the light. Copy reached over and swatted the switch. The light went on.

His face tight with concentration, Paul studied the switch. "You see," he said at last. "The switch is upside down. And it's easy enough for a cat to push."

Beth was amused. Everything looked easy when you knew the answers.

With the mystery completely unravelled, they lingered in the kitchen, talking. Paul, it turned out, liked many of the things Beth did. Especially fish. He raised angels in his basement.

They secured the cats and locked the house.

"Can you come to my house for a few minutes?" Beth asked. "We should figure out how we're going to divide up the cat sitting until the Goodalls come home."

As they ducked under the hedge, they heard a crash from the Carews' garden.

Beth dropped to her knees. "Oh, no! I thought that part was imagination!"

Paul asked, "What did you have for supper?"

"For supper? What's that got to do with anything?"

Paul crept ahead. "Something with bones, I'll bet," he whispered. "Steak?"

72

"Paul Kallin, boy detective," Beth said.

On the other side of the hedge, he motioned her to silence. A dark shape hovered over the garbage can outside the back door, ripping through the garbage.

The outside light came on.

The animal's head snapped up. A raccoon! It chomped down on a bone and dropped out of sight.

Beth shivered, remembering the other-worldly wailing she and her parents had heard. Surely it and the crash were both noises made by raccoons.

"Another creature of the dark unmasked," Beth joked.

"He can see out of his at least," Paul said.

Mr. Carew came out, shaking his head over the mess the raccoon had made.

"I'm glad he didn't make a mess like that the night I heard him at the Goodalls'," Beth said.

"He did. The morning I went fishing. I cleaned it up."

"Frank? What was it?" Mrs. Carew came out. "Oh, Beth, I'm glad you're home."

Beth introduced her to Paul.

"The gardener," Mr. Carew said in recognition.

"Have you known one another long?" Mrs. Carew asked.

Paul and Beth looked at each other like conspirators. After what they'd been through, that was a difficult question to answer.

Beth couldn't resist saying, "In spirit anyway," knowing Paul would get the joke.

Paul flashed her a smile.

Mr. Carew sneezed.

Beth edged toward the door. "Paul raises angel fish. I'm taking him up to see mine. Okay?"

Leading Paul up the kitchen staircase, Beth explained the cracks in the wall and told him how she had figured out the secret of the Goodalls' pantry door. Pieces of different puzzles, and yet everything fitted together.

"I was just lucky we had the house jacked up, or I never would have figured it out."

Beth unhooked her door and turned on the light. Cheepy fluttered a greeting. The fish swam in peaceful circles. The mobiles swung gently overhead. Even the horses on the shelves and the lions on the rug seemed to come alive. Only the four-leaf clovers looked droopy.

That was all right though, because Beth knew luck was something that grew on the inside. It was an attitude, a way of looking at things. Sometimes you had to dig for it, but it was there all right. It was there all the time.

She stepped aside to let Paul in.

"This is *my* room," she said.